This **Aussie Kids** book belongs to

....

who lives in

....

To Poppy. A perfect guide! x *J.B.*
To Daisy and Leilani. See you on the beach! *D.S.*

PUFFIN BOOKS

UK | USA | Canada | Ireland | Australia
India | New Zealand | South Africa | China

Penguin
Random House
Australia

Penguin Random House Australia is part of the Penguin Random House group of
companies whose addresses can be found at global.penguinrandomhouse.com.

First published by Puffin Books, an imprint of
Penguin Random House Australia Pty Ltd, in 2020
Text copyright © Janeen Brian 2020
Illustrations copyright © Danny Snell 2020

Cover and internal illustrations by Danny Snell
Design © Penguin Random House Australia Pty Ltd
Author photograph © Alex Kelly
Typeset in 18pt New Century Schoolbook by Midland Typesetters, Australia

Printed and bound in China

A catalogue record for this
book is available from the
National Library of Australia

ISBN 978 1 76089 366 8

Penguin Random House Australia uses papers that are natural and
recyclable products, made from wood grown in sustainable forests. The logging
and manufacture processes are expected to conform to the environmental
regulations of the country of origin.

penguin.com.au

Aussie Kids

Meet Mia by the Jetty

Janeen Brian
& Danny Snell

PUFFIN BOOKS

Northern
Territory

Western
Australia

South
Australia

Come visit
me in South
Australia

Australia

Queensland

New South Wales

ACT

Victoria

Tasmania

Hi! I'm Mia

POSTCARD

Hi,

I'm Mia. I love living near the beach. There's always lots of great things to do and see. I'm very good at having ideas too. So I never get bored! I'd love you to come and visit. I could show you around. I bet you'd have fun as well!

Mia

FROM:

Mia

Victor Harbor

South Australia

Australia

Chapter 1

A Visitor

My name's Mia. I live at the
beach at Victor Harbor. The
beach is across the road from
my house. I go down a little
path, past bushes and rocks
and then onto the white
sand.

I have sharp eyes and find things in the sand. I've found a big crab claw, a shiny rainbow shell, and a rock that looks like a banana.

From my bed I can hear the waves and smell the salty sea.

I have a big sister called Alice. Alice thinks she's the boss of everyone. But she's not.

One day, Mum said,
'A boy is coming to stay this
weekend. His name is Jim.'

'A *real* boy?' I said. We
don't have many boys come
to our house.

Alice lifted her eyebrows. 'Boys *are* real, Mia.'

'Robot ones aren't,' I said with a sniff. But then I got goosebumps. I'd thought of a very good plan. But I didn't tell Alice.

'Why is Jim coming here?' Alice said.

'He's the son of an old friend,' said Mum. 'She has to go to hospital for a few days. So I said Jim could stay.'

Alice shrugged and looked out the window. I looked out the window too. Granite Island stared back.

It was an island not far from the beach.

Now it was part of my plan
as well. I was going to be a
super tour guide!

Chapter 2

My Plan is So Good

Next day, at school, I told Bibi my plan.

'Will you get money for showing people around?' she asked.

'No,' I said. 'I'll just do it because I have a big heart.'

'Oh,' said Bibi.

'But I need a badge for my job. Do you want to help me make one?'

'No thanks,' said Bibi.

'Okay,' I said.

Back at home that afternoon, I was writing my name on the badge.

Alice crept up behind me. 'What are you doing?' she said.

I slapped my hand down. 'Nothing. You can't see.'

'Jim's here,' called Mum.

I slid the badge into my pocket. Then I raced to the front door. Jim was tall like Alice.

'I'm Mia,' I said to him.
'Alice doesn't know about my
special plan yet. But it's good.'

Jim's eyes went big. He
looked like a scared rabbit.

'It's *really* good,' I said,
nodding. 'You'll like it.'

Mum waved goodbye to Jim's mum. 'Come in, Jim,' said Mum. 'Here's your bedroom. Put your bag there.'

After we had a drink and a snack, Mum said, 'Alice, you and Mia can take Jim to the beach. Show him around.'

Perfect.

I rushed into my bedroom and pinned on my badge.

Then I looked in the mirror.

'Hello,' I said with a grin.
'I'm Mia, the Victor Harbor
Tour Guide.'

Alice rolled her eyes when she saw the badge.

'She made it herself,' she told Jim. 'She's not really a tour guide.'

Jim looked at us.

Alice smiled. Alice *never* smiles at boys.

Chapter 3

How Exciting!

We walked across the road
to the beach.

Jim looked about. 'It's
good,' he said.

'Yes,' I said. 'It's the best.'
A tingle ran up and down
my back.

I could tell I was going to
be very good at my job.

I swept my hand around
like an actress on telly.

'This is Encounter Bay,'
I said. 'Seals and dolphins
swim here. So do we.

Also, we jump over seaweed hills and look for crabs in rockpools. It's a good beach for sandcastles as well.

So, today, we're having a sandcastle competition.

I'll be the judge.'

Alice rolled her eyes again. But when Jim began scooping sand, she did too.

I made a beautiful mermaid.

'Stop now.' I held up my hand like we have to at school.

Alice was making a giant octopus. 'I'm not finished,' she said.

'I'm not either.' Jim's castle had a moat.

The tide was drifting in.
It was washing my mermaid's
tail away. 'We have to finish!'
I said. '*I* think my mermaid
is *very, very* good.'

Alice and Jim didn't look.

'So, I say the mermaid's
the winner.'

'It's not,' said Alice,
turning her head. 'It's only
half a mermaid now anyway.'

Alice said Jim was the
winner.

'Cool,' he said. 'Thanks, Alice.'

'But remember I'm still the tour guide, Jim,' I said.

Ding! Ding!

'It's the tram!' I shouted. 'Quick. Run!'

Jim jumped up. 'What tram?'

'Over there.' I pointed. 'See? A horse pulls it across the jetty to Granite Island. It's the only one in Australia.'

'What? The only horse?'
Jim grinned.

I laughed. 'No. The only
horse-drawn tram. Come on.
Let's go!'

Chapter 4

All Aboard!

We arrived, puffing.

'Mr Gus is the driver today!'
I told Jim. 'I know him.'

'We *both* do, Mia.' Alice
turned to Jim. 'He lives next
door. Sometimes he lets us
ride on –'

'Hello, Mr Gus!' I said, pointing to my badge. 'Can we have a ride today? This is Jim. I'm in charge of showing him around.'

'All right, Mia. Jump aboard.'

The tram is green and yellow and it's a double-decker. We climb the steps to the top.

'Mr Gus rings the bell next,' I said.

'Only when everybody's
aboard, Mia,' said Alice,
taking the seat next to Jim.
'Anyway,' I said, 'I know
the names of the horses.'

'Yes, because they're painted on the side of the tram,' Alice said.

She thinks she knows everything. But she doesn't.

'What's the name of the horse that starts with *M* then?' I asked.

Alice did her eye-roll. 'Murray,' she said. 'Like the river.'

'*Nooo*,' I said. 'I was thinking of *Misty*.'

'They're both good names,'
said Jim. 'My horse is called
Braddy.'

'You've got a horse?' I said.
'A *real* one?'

Jim nodded.

'*Wow!*' Alice opened her
mouth wide. But she just
likes dogs. She's only patted
a horse once in her life.

The bell rang again.
Mr Gus clicked the reins and
the horse set off.

The tram rumbled along the jetty.

Below us, the sea rolled in sparkly waves. The sun was like a warm hug.

'You can see the whole world from up here!' I said.

'Do you ride your horse?' Alice shifted closer to Jim.

'Yes! Mainly on the weekends,' said Jim.

The tram stopped at Granite Island and we clambered down.

'Now,' I said. 'I'll tell you about the island.'

Chapter 5

On the Island!

'Tram leaves in forty
minutes!' called Mr Gus.

I waved because that's
polite. Then I said, 'There
are big rocks on Granite
Island.' I stretched my arms
as far as they would go.

'Big, like giants' fists!
And there are little fairies.'
I grinned at Jim in a secret
way.

Alice sighed. 'She means
Fairy Penguins.'

Jim looked surprised.

'Most go out fishing in the day,' said Alice. 'But –'

'They come back to their burrows at sunset,' I said, in case Alice got it wrong.

'Wow!' said Jim. 'Can we see them?'

'Follow me,' I said. 'But be *very* quiet.'

I crept along a winding path.

'I have sharp eyes,' I told Jim. 'Ah, there! *Shhh.*' On my hands and knees, I peered into a burrow. 'Sometimes there are baby chicks waiting for their parents to return.'

'Are there any in here?' said Jim.

'Yes,' I whispered, 'but don't disturb them. Or flash any light into their eyes. It hurts them and then they can't see.'

'Cool!' said Jim.

'I've seen penguins before,' said Alice.

Chapter 6

Through the Binoculars

A short time later, we rode back across the jetty. The bay curved and houses dotted the shore.

'Thank you, Mr Gus,' I said as we climbed down from the tram.

Then I pointed to a big, brick building nearby. 'That's the Whale Centre.'

'Jim can read, Mia,' said Alice.

'A tour guide *has* to say things, Alice,' I said. 'It's part of their job.'

Alice groaned. 'Do you want to go back home, Jim? We can do something else.'

'He can't,' I said, smiling.

'I'm still being a guide.'

In front of the whale

building was a statue of a

whale tail.

'Where's the rest of the

whale?' The corners of Jim's

mouth twitched.

'It dived underground!'
I said. 'And now it's stuck.
It can never get up again!'
I laughed and laughed.

'As if,' scoffed Alice.

'Hey, Jim,' I said. 'We could
look for *real* whales. I've got
my binoculars.'

'They're plastic, Mia!' said
Alice. 'They help you see ants.'

'Come on, Jim,' I said.
'There's a cliff close by.
People look for whales there.'

'Okay.'

Alice folded her arms. '*All right*,' she moaned.

A family was already at the cliff spot.

'Hello,' I said. Then I squinted through my binoculars.

'Can you see anything?' asked Jim.

'Mmm . . .' I began.

'*A sailor went to sea, sea, sea, to see what he could see, see, see,*' chanted Alice.

I pulled a face.

But then I saw something. What was it?

Chapter 7

Guess What?

'A whale!' I cried. 'It's a whale!'

'Where? Where?' Alice pulled the binoculars from me.

'Can you see it? Can you see it?' I cried.

Alice's mouth opened. She burst out laughing.

'It's a boat, Mia! You thought a *boat* was a whale!' Alice went on laughing in a mean way. Then she grinned at Jim.

I looked down and blinked
hard. There was a rushing
sound in my ears and my
heart thumped like a loud
drum.

'But there *is* a whale!' cried the mum in the family. 'Look, Danny!' She handed her binoculars to the dad. 'See? Out there where that little girl was looking.'

Did she mean me? I held my breath.

'Yes!' cried the dad. 'You're right. It *is* a whale!'

The kids jumped up and down.

'Whale! Whale! Can we look, Dad? Hurry, please.'

The mum turned and smiled at me. 'I wouldn't have seen it if I hadn't been watching you,' she said. 'Not everyone gets to see a whale!'

Later, she let Jim, Alice and me look through her special binoculars.

We saw the whale leap and dive and blow water out its spout. WOW!

'That was so good,' said Jim as we walked home.

And when the wind twisted my badge back-to-front, Alice fixed it for me.

It was the best day ever.

And guess what? Tomorrow, there's the Cockle Train and the camel rides. I can be Mia, the Tour Guide again!

Fun Facts
About Fairy Penguins

There are 17 kinds of penguins,
but the Fairy Penguin is the smallest.

Fairy Penguins live in
the cold seas in the
south of Australia
and New Zealand but
their feathers keep
them warm.

About the AUTHOR

I've always lived by
the sea. And always
loved jetties! On a jetty, I could
walk out further than I could swim.
I could also look into the deep
green waters and wonder about
the sea world below. But when
I was little, I was scared I might
slip through the gaps in the wooden
planks! I didn't. ☀

About the ILLUSTRATOR

I've always lived in Adelaide. It's a great city with many beautiful beaches to choose from. My two daughters love swimming and we often find ourselves heading to Victor Harbor and the beaches on the southern coast to swim and explore. ☺

Tick the Aussie Kids books you have read:

Meet Mia by the Jetty
Janeen Brian & Danny Snell

Meet Taj at the Lighthouse
Maxine Beneba Clarke & Nicki Greenberg

Meet Zoe and Zac at the Zoo
Belinda Murrell & David Hardy

Meet Eve in the Outback
Raewyn Caisley & Karen Blair

Meet Katie at the Beach
Rebecca Johnson & Lucia Masciullo

Meet Sam at the Mangrove Creek
Paul Seden & Brenton McKenna

Meet Dooley on the Farm
Sally Odgers & Christina Booth

Meet Matilda at the Festival
Jacqueline de Rose-Ahern & Tania McCartney